Thing-Thing

Cary Fagan • Nicolas Debon

EXCELSIOR

TUNDRA BOOKS

TEXT COPYRIGHT © 2008 BY CARY FAGAN
ILLUSTRATIONS COPYRIGHT © 2008 BY NICOLAS DEBON

Published in Canada by Tundra Books,
75 Sherbourne Street, Toronto, Ontario M5A 2P9

Published in the United States by Tundra Books of Northern New York,
P.O. Box 1030, Plattsburgh, New York 12901

LIBRARY OF CONGRESS CONTROL NUMBER: 2007906496

LIBRARY AND ARCHIVES CANADA CATALOGUING IN PUBLICATION
·

Fagan, Cary
Thing-Thing / Cary Fagan ; illustrated by Nicolas Debon.
ISBN 978-0-88776-839-2
I. Debon, Nicolas, 1968- II. Title.
PS8561.A375T48 2008   jC813'.54   C2007-905364-5

We acknowledge the financial support of the Government of Canada through the Book Publishing Industry
Development Program (BPIDP) and that of the Government of Ontario through the Ontario Media Development
Corporation's Ontario Book Initiative.
We further acknowledge the support of the Canada Council for the Arts and the Ontario Arts Council for our
publishing program.

ONTARIO ARTS COUNCIL
CONSEIL DES ARTS DE L'ONTARIO

The illustrations for this book were rendered in gouache on Arches paper

Typeset in Kosmik
Printed and bound in China

1 2 3 4 5 6   13 12 11 10 09 08

For my mother, Belle Fagan, who first read to me.

Today was Archibald Crimp's birthday and Archibald Crimp was in a very bad mood.

His parents had taken him on a special weekend trip to the city. Archibald sat in the bed of their hotel room on the sixth floor of the Excelsior Hotel. All around him were birthday presents — electronic games and racing car sets, remote-control robots and space vehicles, a plastic set of armor, and much, much more. But not one of the presents had pleased him.

"These are just like the toys I already have," Archibald said. "I'm not getting out of this bed until you bring me something I like."

So Archibald Crimp's father

ran to the enormous toy store at the
end of the street to search for something
his son did not already own.

There was nothing in the games
department, nothing in the dinosaur section,
nothing even on the magic tricks display. He
trudged back through the store, thinking of
how awful it would be to return empty-handed.

Then, he saw something high on a shelf.
He stretched up on his toes and brought it down.

Archibald Crimp already had many stuffed
animals, but this one was different. What kind of animal
was it exactly? Not quite a bunny rabbit, but not quite
a dog either, nor a bear, or cat for that matter.

Archibald's father looked at the little tag on the foot
of the animal. The tag read:

Thing-Thing

It wasn't very expensive. Archibald preferred expensive toys. Hoping
for the best, his father bought it anyway.

"Look, Archie-kins," said Mr. Crimp, as he rushed into the room on the sixth floor of the Excelsior Hotel.

"Oh, what is it?" said Mrs. Crimp. "Open the box, Sweetness."

Archibald Crimp took the box and tore off the wrapping. He looked inside and made a sour face.

"This isn't any real sort of animal at all," he said.

"But you don't have one like it," his father said in a pleading tone.

"And I don't want one! This is the worst present of them all!"

And with that, Archibald picked up
Thing-Thing and threw it. He threw it right
across the room and out the open window.

Oh dear, thought Thing-Thing to itself. *This is bad, this is very bad*

At the store, Thing-Thing had heard rumors about such children, but he hadn't believed them to be true. Thing-Thing hadn't wanted them to be true. It had hoped to be given to a child who would love it, and talk to it, and make it tea parties, and dress it up, and hang onto it when sad or lonely, and get it sticky with jam, and take it to bed.

Instead, Thing-Thing, feeling very sorry for itself, had been thrown out a window.

And was falling.

Staying on the floor below – the fifth floor – was a hockey player named Isabel. Isabel played right wing for a team called the Warburton Redwings. That very day the Warburton Redwings were going to play in the championship game against the Strassburg Stingers.

Isabel had hurt her ankle.

She hadn't hurt it playing hockey. She had twisted it playing hopscotch with her little brother.

"You mean I can't play?" she asked.

"No," said the team doctor. "Your ankle needs to rest."

Tears welled in Isabel's eyes. She didn't want the coach and the doctor to see her cry, so she turned her face to the window. And noticed something: a stuffed animal falling past.

That's strange, thought Isabel. It made her think of her little brother. Her little brother had a favorite stuffed kangaroo that he dragged with him wherever he went.

Well, at least when her ankle got better she could play hopscotch and hockey again.

It's a very strange feeling, falling through the air,

thought Thing-Thing. Sometimes it was ears-down and

sometimes it was ears-up and sometimes it was sideways.

Thing-Thing wasn't scared. Well, maybe just a little...

On the window ledge rested a bird's nest. A robin's nest

in fact, with a mother robin just turning over two

of the loveliest blue eggs you ever saw.

But Thing-Thing had already fallen past.

On the next floor below – the fourth floor – a man in a brown suit was making a speech in the hotel meeting room.

"This is our fantastic new product, the Boomer 2000," said the man in the brown suit. He was holding up the Boomer 2000. It was made of plastic and had a lot of switches. It required seventeen batteries.

"We must sell the Boomer 2000 until there is one in every house!" shouted the man in the brown suit. "We must get out there and sell, sell, sell!"

Behind the man in the brown suit was a window. At that moment something fell past it.

"Did you see that?" whispered a young man sitting in the front row.

"I think it was a stuffed squirrel," said the woman beside him.

"No, I think it was a stuffed bat," said the man on the other side.

"Whatever it was," said the man in the middle, "I bet it doesn't need seventeen batteries."

At least, thought Thing-Thing,

who always tried to look on the bright side,

...It's a nice day out there.

One floor below – the third floor – was the hotel dining room. At a table by the window, a very, very old woman was eating her lunch. Her name was Matilda Rusk. Her children were grown up now and had moved away.

Matilda Rusk liked to read poetry while she ate her lunch. She was just reading the line Hope is the thing with feathers, when something caught her eye and made her look up.

Matilda Rusk said something out loud. She said, "Foo-Foo." Foo-Foo had been her favorite stuffed animal when she was a child a long, long time ago. It had been made for her by her mother.

"Did you want something?" asked the waiter, who had been passing by.

"No, nothing," said Matilda Rusk softly. "Nothing at all."

A kindly old woman, thought Thing-Thing. But I would prefer a younger owner.

A spider was spinning a web under a stone gargoyle. "Look out for the ground!" called the spider.

But I can't really look out for the ground, thought Thing-Thing. It is more like the ground should look out for me.

On the floor below – the second floor – a nervous young man was down on his knee before a young woman.

"Bethany," the man said passionately, clasping the young woman's hand. "Will you . . . will you marry me?"

Bethany surprised the young man by getting down on her knee.

"Alex," she said, "will you marry me?"

"Why, yes, of course. Of course I will!"

"Good," said the young woman and she leaned forward and kissed him. The young man closed his eyes for a moment. When he opened them again, he saw a fuzzy creature plunge past the window.

"I'm so happy," the young man said, "that I'm seeing things."

Congratulations, and many happy returns! thought Thing-Thing, *Whatever that means.* Thing-Thing looked down.

oh my. Oh my, oh my,
Oh my!
Thing-Thing's little heart pounded.

On the floor below that – the ground floor – was the lobby of the Excelsior Hotel. As always, it was bustling with some people arriving and other people leaving. A bellhop carried flowers, a news vendor sold his papers, and nobody at all bothered to look out the window.

So nobody saw a stuffed animal that wasn't quite a rabbit and wasn't quite a bear, dropping past the window.

And nobody saw the baby carriage coming along the sidewalk. The man and the woman pushing the carriage were very tired because the baby had woken up so many times during the night. They had hoped that a stroll in the park would stop their baby from crying. It hadn't.

Nobody saw the stuffed animal fall into the carriage and thump gently onto the blanket.

Nobody except the baby.

The couple pushed the carriage into the hotel. They passed the people arriving and the people leaving, the messenger with flowers, and the newspaper seller.

They stopped in front of the elevator, and pressed the button. They waited.

The elevator door opened. There stood Archibald Crimp with his parents. Archibald had a scowl on his face because he did not want to go out. As he left the elevator, he looked into the carriage.

"Hey!" he cried. "That's my toy!"

"You," said Archibald's father, "have quite enough toys. Now come along to the park. What you need is some fresh air. What you need is some fun."

Archibald's parents pulled him away.

The man and the woman pushed the carriage into the elevator. Surprised, they looked at one another, for they had just realized the same thing at the same time.

Their baby wasn't crying anymore.

Thing-Thing had felt the thump as it landed.

How lucky, he thought. I've landed on something soft. It seems to be a blanket.

Now Thing-Thing felt something else. It felt five little fingers stroking its ear. It felt those fingers close on its ear and pull it closer.

The next thing it knew, Thing-Thing was staring into the very large eyes of a baby.

"Hello. Would you like me to belong to you?" asked Thing-Thing.

"Ahh-mummmm-oooo," said the baby, pulling Thing-Thing even closer. Thing-Thing felt a surge of happiness. "I think," he said, "why, I think that means yes."